A Blue's Clues Holiday

Blue's Clues

W9-BYD-047

by Angela C. Santomero

illustrated by Yo-Lynn Hagood

SCHOLASTIC INC.

New York Toronto London Auckland Sydney
Mexico City New Delhi Hong Kong

Blue! Look who's here to share in our family traditions! Everyone is making something to add to our holiday decorations. Will you help us finish our decorations? You will? Great.

Paper chains! Blue makes her paper chains every year to hang around the house. Can you help her? We just need to cut some construction paper into long strips, then we use some glue to connect the strips into a circle.

Yum! Mr. Salt and Mrs. Pepper always bake the most yummy holiday cookies! Do you know what shape the cookies are?

2 CUPS FLOUR

2 CUPS PECANS

1 CUP BUTTER

4 TBSP. SUGAR

DASH SALT

1 TSP. VANILLA

MIX

ROLL

BAKE

350°

25

SPRINKLES

SUGAR

SPRINKLE

Mr. Salt and Mrs. Pepper's snowball cookies are easy to make. Maybe you can make some for your family too. Hey, let's see what Shovel and Pail are up to!

Shovel and Pail are making paper snowflakes to decorate our living room. Aren't they pretty?

Hey, maybe you want to try to make paper snowflakes too!

Look at Slippery! He's making something festive out of bubbles to put in our room. What did he make? Can you tell?

Hey, Tickety! Did you make something too? What did Tickety make this year?

This is my favorite part of our holiday. Now we go to each of our friends' houses and give each of them a holiday present. Will you sing your favorite holiday song for us as we walk? Great.

Here we are at the first house on our stop. Do you know whose house this is? It's Green Puppy's house! I wonder what holiday they are celebrating? Do you know?

I'm so excited because Green Puppy said that green blocks are her favorite! Here we are at our second house. Do you know whose house this is? It's Orange Kitten's house, Blue's friend from school! Do you know what holiday they are celebrating?

They are celebrating Hanukkah! Hanukkah is the holiday when people celebrate the miracle of light. Wow, that's so nice. Oh, I almost forgot. We brought something special for Orange Kitten, too. And look, it is her favorite color!

This is my favorite part: visiting with our friends. Oh! Here we are at our last stop on our trip through the neighborhood. Whose house do you think this is? It's Purple Kangaroo's house! Do you know what they are celebrating?

Okay, now that we are back home, it's time for us to give out our last two presents. We have a magenta-colored painter's outfit left in our bag. Who do you think that could be for?